WAKEBOARDING

BY HOLLIE ENDRES

BELLWETHER MEDIA • MINNEAPOLIS, MN

TORQUE™

Are you ready to take it to the extreme?
Torque books thrust you into the action-packed world
of sports, vehicles, and adventure. These books may
include dirt, smoke, fire, and dangerous stunts.
WARNING: read at your own risk.

This edition first published in 2008 by Bellwether Media.

No part of this publication may be reproduced in whole or in part without written
permission of the publisher. For information regarding permission, write to Bellwether
Media Inc., Attention: Permissions Department, Post Office Box 1C, Minnetonka, MN
55345-9998.

Library of Congress Cataloging-in-Publication Data

Endres, Hollie J.
Wakeboarding / by Hollie Endres.
      p. cm. -- (Torque : action sports)
Summary: "Photographs of amazing feats accompany engaging information about
wakeboarding. The combination of high-interest subject matter and light text
is intended to engage readers in grades three through seven"--Provided by
publisher.
Includes bibliographical references and index.
ISBN-13: 978-1-60014-129-4 (hardcover : alk. paper)
ISBN-10: 1-60014-129-3 (hardcover : alk. paper)
1. Wakeboarding--Juvenile literature. I. Title.

GV840.W34E53 2008
797.3--dc22   2007021128

Text copyright © 2008 by Bellwether Media.

CONTENTS

RIDING THE WAKE   4

WHAT IS WAKEBOARDING? 8

EQUIPMENT   12

IN ACTION   16

GLOSSARY   22

TO LEARN MORE   23

INDEX   24

RIDING THE WAKE

A speedboat slices across the calm water. Two long waves form a narrow V-shaped **wake** behind the boat. A single wakeboarder darts back and forth across the wake.

The wakeboarder is ready to do a trick. He gives the **towrope** a hard tug and cuts to the left. The board launches into the air as it hits the wake. The wakeboarder swings his board up and out behind him. He lands perfectly. He has just landed a heelside **raley**!

WHAT IS WAKEBOARDING?

Wakeboarding is a mix of waterskiing, surfing, and snowboarding. Wakeboarders are towed behind a boat like waterskiers. They ride along the wake the boat creates like surfers on a wave. Their jumps, flips, and grabs look like snowboarding tricks.

Wakeboarding grew out of a sport called **skurfing**. Skurfing was popular in the 1980s. Skurfers rode surfboard-like boards behind boats. Riders soon added **bindings** to hold their feet to the boards and give them better control. This became the sport of wakeboarding.

Wakeboards are built for doing tricks. They are light and strong. Their ends are slightly raised so they don't dip into the water as the rider slices and turns.

Fins on the bottom of a board help it cut cleanly through the water. A wakeboarder's feet are strapped into bindings. These straps attach to the top of the board.

Wakeboarders need more than just a board. They also need a powerful boat, a good driver, and a stiff towrope. Professional riders always wear helmcts and life jackets to protect themselves during **wipeouts**.

Many wakeboarders like to compete in freestyle events. The wakeboarders have a set amount of time to land as many tricks as they can. They earn points from judges for exciting tricks and clean landings.

Wakeboarders perform all kinds of tricks. A roll is a trick in which a rider hits the wake and rolls the board sideways all the way around in the air. Flips and board grabs are also popular. **Surface 360s** are full spins on the surface of the water.

Wakeboarders combine these tricks in exciting ways. They're always coming up with new tricks to keep the fans on their feet.

GLOSSARY

bindings—straps that keep a wakeboarder's feet attached to the board

raley—a trick where wakeboarders hit the wake and allow their bodies to swing backwards, parallel to the water

skurfing—a sport in which riders are towed on surfboard-like boards behind a boat; skurfers do not have bindings to attach their feet to the board.

surface 360—a full spin done on the surface of the water without using the wake to jump

towrope—a rope attached to the boat; wakeboarders hold on to the towrope when they are pulled.

wake—the V-shaped wave created by a moving boat

wipeout—a crash or fall

TO LEARN MORE

AT THE LIBRARY

Blomquist, Christopher. *Wakeboarding in the X Games*. New York: PowerKids Press, 2003.

Kalman, Bobbie. *Extreme Wakeboarding*. New York: Crabtree Pub. Co., 2006.

Peterson, Christine. *Wakeboarding*. Mankato, Minn.: Capstone Press, 2005.

ON THE WEB

Learning more about wakeboarding is as easy as 1, 2, 3.

1. Go to www.factsurfer.com
2. Enter "wakeboarding" into search box.
3. Click the "Surf" button and you will see a list of related web sites.

With factsurfer.com, finding more information is just a click away.

INDEX

1980s, 10
1996, 7
bindings, 10, 13
boat, 5, 8, 10, 15
Bonifay, Parks, 19
driver, 11, 15
fans, 21
fins, 13
freestyle events, 17
grab, 8, 18
jumps, 8
life jackets, 15

raley, 6
roll, 18
safety, 15
skurfing, 10
snowboarding, 8
surfing, 8
towrope, 6, 15
wake, 5, 6, 8, 18
waterskiing, 8
wipeouts, 15
X Games, 7